Off
Market

Om
KIDZ
An imprint of **Om** Books International

 **Om Books International**

Reprinted in 2018

Corporate & Editorial Office
A-12, Sector 64, Noida 201 301
Uttar Pradesh, India
Phone: +91 120 477 4100
Email: editorial@ombooks.com
Website: www.ombooksinternational.com

Sales Office
107, Ansari Road, Darya Ganj
New Delhi 110 002, India
Phone: +91 11 4000 9000
Email: sales@ombooks.com
Website: www.ombooks.com

© Om Books International 2017

ISBN: 978-93-86108-90-6

Printed in India

10 9 8 7 6 5 4 3 2

Off to the
Market

Paste your
photograph here

My name is

_____

It's a **hot**, summer **day**.
Meg is at home.
She tells **her** mother,
"**Mum**, **let**'s make an
apple **pie**!"

Mum does **not** have **all** that **she** needs to make a **pie**. "**Let** us go to **the** market," **she** tells **Meg**. **Meg** is happy to go.

Mum and Meg take **the bus**.
The market is an hour away.
They chat **all the way** there.

Mum and Meg go to **the** fruit shop first. "I want to **buy** apples **and** figs," **Mum** tells **the** shopkeeper.

"Figs?" asks **Meg**.

"To make some **fig jam**," says **Mum**.

Mum and Meg buy the fruits. They go to another shop. "I would like some flour, **and** an **egg** carton," says **Mum**. **The** shopkeeper gives **her** a **bag** of flour **and** a carton of eggs.

"I also need a bottle of **oil and** a packet of **tea** leaves," adds **Mum**.

"We don't need that **for the pie!**" says **Meg**.

Mum smiles. "I need them to
make other things, **Meg**," **she**
explains. **Meg** nods **her** head.
She helps **Mum** carry **the bag**.

They go to **the** last shop.
"I would like to **buy two**
cartons of milk," **Mum** tells
the shopkeeper. **She** opens **her**
bag to **pay the** shopkeeper.

Uh oh! **Mum**'s wallet is missing!
"Where could it go?" says **Mum**.
"I just **had** it!" **Mum** looks
everywhere. **Meg** looks **too**.
Then, **she** remembers.

"**Mum**! I think **you** left it at **the tea** shop," says **Meg**. "**Let** me **run** there **and get** it **for you**."

Meg goes to **the tea** shop. **The** shopkeeper **has Mum**'s wallet. He gives it to **Meg**. **Meg** thanks **him and** takes it to **Mum**.

"Phew!" **Mum** pays **the** shopkeeper. **She** is happy to **get her** wallet back. **Meg and Mum** take **the bus** back home.

Mum makes a delicious apple **pie**.
Meg and Mum eat the pie.
What a lovely **day** they have **had**!

Circle the three-letter words in the shop below.

flour oil

tea egg

jam can

apple

book fig at

Help Meg find the wallet by tracing a path through the maze.

Change just one letter in each word to make a new word. Fill up the ladders with new words.

JAM
DAM
DAD
HAD
HAY

FIG

SUN

TEA

Know your words

Sight Words

hot	all	had	let
day	the	too	two
she	way	get	has
her	and	you	
not	for	him	

Naming Words

Meg	bus	egg	oil
Mum	fig	bag	tea
pie	jam		

Doing Words

buy	run	eat
pay